VIKING
ADVENTURES

OOLAF
AND THE
GOLDEN BOOK

Written and Illustrated by Andy Elkerton

W
FRANKLIN WATTS
LONDON•SYDNEY

Chapter One

Chief Forkbeard, Jarl of the Village at the End of the World, untied the top of the heavy sack and emptied everything out. "What an adventure!" he laughed.

Forkbeard had been away for many months.

He had brought back lots of amazing things.

"Just look at this helmet ... and this goblet!"

he said, picking them up, proudly.

"What's this, Dad?" asked Oolaf, spotting
a dusty old book. Its pages were locked
by a golden clasp.

"I don't remember this," said Forkbeard. He
tried to open the clasp but it wouldn't budge.

"It's no use if it won't open. Throw it out!"

"Can I have it?" asked Oolaf.

Oolaf took the book and raced down the street towards a rickety little house with a grassy roof. Wisps of smoke curled up from the gaps between the turf. He knocked on the door. Skald, the Village Storyteller, peeked out.

6

"This is very strange indeed, Oolaf," said Skald, taking the book. "Perhaps someone doesn't want us to know what secrets are inside ..." he said, pushing and poking the clasp, "... but I can fix that." Suddenly, the clasp popped apart and the book creaked open.

POP!

7

The two of them gasped. The pages were filled with beautiful pictures and patterns that glittered in the lamplight. The strange letters shone like gold.

"These are runes," gasped Skald, "Letters that were given to us by the gods!"

8

He scratched his chin, and his brow went wrinkly. Oolaf knew Skald was thinking very hard indeed.

"What I think you have here, my boy, is a magic book!" Skald concluded.

"Thanks, Skald!" Oolaf beamed.

He took the book and ran home.

Chapter Two

That night, Oolaf sat in his bed with the book on his lap. The pages were filled with pictures of all sorts of magical things – a huge tree, a rainbow bridge, a dragon and an eagle. On the very last page was an old man with a single, beady eye. Oolaf read on until he started to feel sleepy.

He woke with a start. His bedroom had gone!
He was in a small, dark room. In the
corner was an old man hunched on a chair.
He had a wide-brimmed hat, and a black
raven on each shoulder.

Oolaf didn't dare move.
He didn't dare breathe.

"I've been waiting for you, Oolaf Oolafson,"
said the man. "How do you like my book?"
"I like it very much," gulped Oolaf.
The old man jumped up from his chair.
"What a relief!" He bounded over to Oolaf
and bowed low. "Pleased to meet you.
My name is Odin." Oolaf gasped. This little
old man was king of the Norse gods!

"If you're wondering why you're here, it's all because of the book," Odin continued. "I put a spell on it, to find somebody clever and brave who'd look after the stories inside, and never forget them."

"I hope you'll look after it, Oolaf," Odin said. "Learn your runes, and tell these fantastic tales to everyone. But first, let's see if you're up to the task." Then he gave a wink, clicked his fingers, and disappeared in a flash.

Chapter Three

Oolaf gasped. He was now sitting in the branches of a huge tree. Far below him were clouds, mountains and distant lands. Oolaf knew *exactly* where he was.

Skald had told him stories about this place.
This was the great tree **Yggdrasil**. It held
all the Viking worlds safely in its branches,
including the village where Oolaf lived.

Oolaf sighed. Getting down seemed impossible. He might be stuck there forever! Then, a squirrel suddenly appeared. The squirrel's job was to run up and down the tree taking messages between Nidhogg the dragon and the great eagle.

Seeing the squirrel gave Oolaf a clever idea.

"I've got a message for the eagle," he said.

"It's a secret message that's just for him!"

The squirrel scampered off. Soon,

a giant bird appeared overhead.

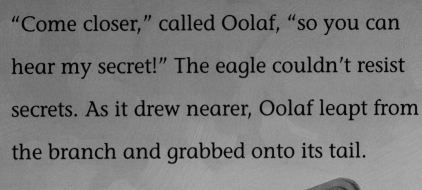

"Come closer," called Oolaf, "so you can hear my secret!" The eagle couldn't resist secrets. As it drew nearer, Oolaf leapt from the branch and grabbed onto its tail.

The furious bird squawked and screeched as it tumbled through the sky. Oolaf soon found himself falling, a giant tail feather clasped in his hands.

Oolaf quickly held the feather over his head and began to glide gently through the air. As he glided, he spotted a rainbow below. "That looks like a safe place to land," he thought, and he steered himself towards it.

Chapter Four

But Oolaf had never stood on a rainbow before. He didn't realise just how slippery they could be. As he landed, he went sliding off along the colours!

He spotted a distant world below. There were tiny boats bobbing on an icy sea, a village of tiny houses and even tinier people. "That's my home!" he exclaimed. He'd go whizzing past if he didn't do something – and quick! Nidhogg was waiting at the end of the rainbow, licking his scaly lips.

Oolaf flapped his arms and dug his feet in but he couldn't slow down. He tried using the feather like a rudder, but that just made him go faster. He sailed right over his village.

Oolaf closed his eyes and fell right into Nidhogg's greedy mouth, still holding the feather. The dragon snapped its jaws shut.

But the feather tickled the dragon's throat.

A second later it spat Oolaf back out again.

Oolaf sailed over his own village once more and began falling downward. He was heading straight towards home. Lower and lower he fell, until it looked like he was going to crash through the roof of his bedroom. "Aieeeeeeee!"

Chapter Five

Oolaf woke with a start! The morning sun was shining through the window and the golden book was still on his lap. He wondered if it had all been a dream.

Then Oolaf remembered what Odin had said. He looked in the book. On the very last page, right beside the old man, was a picture of himself holding a golden book!

Oolaf tucked the book under his arm and raced down the street to a rickety little house with a grassy roof. He knocked on the door. Skald peeked out.

Kaaaaaw
Kaaaaaw

"Skald!" said Oolaf excitedly,

"Have I got a story for you!"

31

Viking mythology and glossary

Eagle

A great eagle was thought to have lived
in the branches of Yggdrasil.

Nidhogg

The name of the fierce dragon believed
to have lived in the roots of Yggdrasil.

Odin

In Norse mythology, Odin was the father of all
Nordic gods. It was thought he had two ravens,
which sat on each shoulder.

Runes

Series of letters that Vikings and Anglo Saxons
used like an alphabet to form messages.

Yggdrasil

A mythical sacred ash tree, also known as
the Tree of Life, which the Vikings thought
held all the different worlds together.